W9-CUW-516

EARTHQUAKES
A PRACTICAL SURVIVAL GUIDE

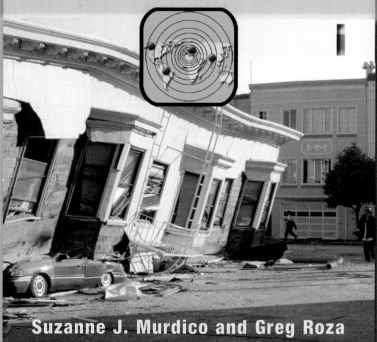

Suzanne J. Murdico and Greg Roza

rosen
central™

The Rosen Publishing Group, Inc., New York

Published in 2006 by The Rosen Publishing Group, Inc.
29 East 21st Street, New York, NY 10010

Copyright © 2006 by The Rosen Publishing Group, Inc.

First Edition

Library of Congress Cataloging-in-Publication Data

Murdico, Suzanne J.
Earthquakes: a practical survival guide / Suzanne J. Murdico and Greg Roza.
    p. cm.—(The library of emergency preparedness)
Includes bibliographical references and index.
ISBN 1-4042-0531-4 (library binding)
1. Earthquakes—Juvenile literature. 2. Emergency management—Juvenile literature. I. Roza, Greg. II. Title. III. Series.
HV599.M87 2006
363.34'95–dc22

                               2005017632

Manufactured in Malaysia

On the cover: In 1989, an earthquake in San Francisco, California, shook an apartment building off its foundation, and caused it to collapse on a car. Engineers and architects are developing new techniques, such as placing rubber and steel between a building and its foundation, for making structures more earthquake resistant than older masonry buildings.

CONTENTS

Introduction

It happened in the early morning hours of January 17, 1994. Like millions of other people living in Los Angeles, California, Ian Brown was fast asleep. The first sound, at 4:31 AM, was the jingling of metal drawer handles throughout the house. Brown was familiar with this sound. As he was jolted awake, he thought, it's just an earthquake.

Having lived in California for four years, Brown had experienced earthquakes before. At first, he wasn't concerned. As he explained in his personal account in *Saturday Night* magazine, those previous quakes had been minor blips on the radar. "We thought: earthquake!" he wrote. "Then we proceeded with our lives as if nothing had happened, our mortality barely dented."

This earthquake was different from the others, though. Instead of dying down, the vibrations grew more intense. Within five seconds, the bed was shifting from side to side—a foot (0.3 meters) each way. Brown struggled just to keep from rolling off the bed. His first instinct was to locate a doorway to stand in. He had heard that a doorway was a safe place to be during an earthquake. In the days that followed, however, he learned that doorways are actually not stronger than any other parts of the structure. They are no longer recommended as a safe location.

A resident of Grenada Hills in Los Angeles, California, surveyed what remained of his home after an earthquake struck Southern California on January 17, 1994. The earthquake, which became known as the Northridge earthquake, was the most costly quake in U.S. history, causing about $20 billion in total property damage. This quake caused insurance companies in California to pay out more money in claims than the amount they had collected in earthquake premiums over the previous thirty years.

As the earthquake shook his home, Ian Brown remained calm. Things seemed to be happening in slow motion. As he glanced out the window, he noticed an eerie blackness. The electricity had gone out, and the streetlights were dark. "The tremors made their way over west Los Angeles from the north," Brown wrote, "rippling the crust of the earth as they passed. The land became the sea." The shock waves caused transformer stations to malfunction and cables and wires to break, leaving the city in complete darkness.

Brown picked up his infant daughter and tucked her under his arm. The house was shaking up and down now, and he could barely stay standing. Amid the shaking, he careened across the room into a wall, still holding on to his daughter. After only ten seconds had elapsed from the start of the quake, Brown made it to a doorway with his daughter and his wife. As the family of three waited and worried, the ground continued to shake for another twenty seconds.

During that time, Ian Brown thought about the difference between earthquakes and many other natural disasters. Some disasters, such as floods, fires, and blizzards, can be avoided. Earthquakes cannot. "No one can avoid the earth ... not when it is a giant that has picked up your home like a tiny bank and is shaking it for loose change," Brown wrote.

For Ian Brown, the worst part of waiting for the earthquake to end was the noise. He listened to the twisting and creaking of the wooden beams and joints holding together his home. In his written account, he compared the earthquake's sound to "a vast sheet of cellophane being screwed into a ball." Brown then watched as cracks of 2 and 3 feet (0.6 to 0.9 m) in length spread across his living-room wall.

Finally, the earth stopped shaking. Total elapsed time: thirty seconds. The noise finally stopped, too. Brown recalled, "In the silence, I realized how noisy an earthquake is, how terrifying the sound is all by itself." The silence was soon broken by the sounds of car alarms blaring and dogs barking outside.

Although the earthquake had ended, the aftershocks were just beginning. Ian Brown and his family were safe, though. They surveyed the damage and began cleaning up the broken glass and sesame seeds that were strewn about the kitchen. Books had fallen from bookshelves and

🌐 Quake Trivia 🌐

The largest recorded earthquake in the world struck Chile on May 22, 1960. It had a magnitude of 9.5.

The largest recorded earthquake in the United States hit Prince William Sound, Alaska, on March 28, 1964. It had a magnitude of 9.2.

Southern California experiences about 10,000 earthquakes every year. The majority of these quakes are so tiny that no one even notices. Only a few hundred have a magnitude greater than 3.0, and just fifteen to twenty have a magnitude greater than 4.0.

Between 1975 and 1995, only four states—Florida, Iowa, North Dakota, and Wisconsin—had no earthquakes.

The two states in the United Stares that have the fewest earthquakes are Florida and North Dakota.

Source: U.S. Geological Survey

plates from cupboards. As the aftershocks continued, they turned on a portable radio and listened to local earthquake reports.

In those early morning hours, the Brown family sat at their kitchen table. They reflected on their experience, and they stayed very still "as if we were trying to appreciate stillness now that we knew what it was not to have it," wrote Brown. In the hours and days that followed, the Browns would discover that they had survived a major earthquake. The Northridge earthquake of January 17, 1994, had a 6.7 magnitude. It injured thousands and caused sixty deaths and billions of dollars in damage.

MAJOR U.S. EARTHQUAKES

Location	Date and Time	Magnitude and Duration	Number of Deaths	Number of Injuries	Property Damage*
Northridge, California	January 17, 1994, 4:31 AM	6.7 30 seconds	60	9,000	$20 billion
Loma Prieta, California	October 17, 1989, 5:04 PM	7.1 15 seconds	66	3,757	$6 billion
Prince William Sound, Alaska	March 28, 1964, 5:36 PM	9.2 3-4 minutes	131	unknown	$300 million
San Francisco, California	April 18, 1906, 5:12 AM	8.25 40 seconds	about 3,000	unknown	$500 million

* Dollar amounts given in values from that year

Earthquakes like this one can be scary. They are danger-ous and destructive. Earthquakes can strike anywhere at any time and without any warning. Keep in mind, though, that knowledge is power. In this book, you will find out when, where, and why earthquakes occur. More important, you will learn about the essential steps to take before, dur-ing, and after an earthquake strikes. Being prepared is the best defense against the destructive power of earthquakes. This vital knowledge will help you and your family mem-bers stay safe.

1 --- Earthquakes 101

When you think about earthquakes, what do you envision? Maybe you imagine a giant gaping hole in the earth that swallows up everything in its wake, including people, cars, and even buildings. Perhaps you picture the state of California breaking off and falling into the Pacific Ocean. Although either of these scenarios might make an exciting action movie, they are not realistic images of what really happens during an earthquake. One thing is certain, though: earthquakes are among nature's most powerful forces.

Explaining Earthquakes

What is an earthquake? Why do earthquakes occur? An earthquake is a sudden, violent shaking of the ground. The breaking and shifting of large sections of rock beneath Earth's surface cause earthquakes. Scientists have developed a theory, known as plate tectonics, that explains the occurrence of most earthquakes. The forces of plate tectonics have been shaping Earth for hundreds of millions of years.

Earth's surface is made up of huge plates that move under, over, and past one another. The place where these plates slide past one another beneath Earth's surface is called a fault. Usually, this movement is slow and continuous. Sometimes, however, the plates become locked together. Because they cannot move, pressure builds up.

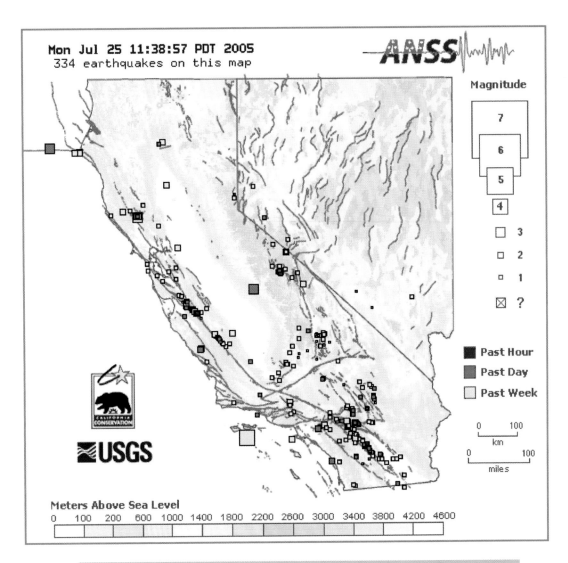

This map, compiled by the U.S. Geological Survey (USGS), depicts the earthquake activity for July 25, 2005, in California and Nevada. The USGS's Web site (http://earthquake.usgs.gov) provides up-to-the-minute information on earthquakes and fault activity throughout the United States.

When the pressure becomes strong enough, the plates break apart, causing the ground to shake. The point along the fault where the plates first break apart is called the focus. Directly above the focus, on Earth's surface, is the epicenter—the place where the earthquake begins.

Earthquake Dangers

Earthquakes can range from minor to moderate to severe. Most minor earthquakes are barely detectable. Even if they are noticeable, they might feel like the rumble of a truck passing by. Moderate quakes can cause some damage, but it is generally not extensive. Severe earthquakes are the greatest cause for concern. These earthquakes can be extremely destructive, especially if they strike cities or other heavily populated areas.

Major earthquakes can cause buildings and bridges to collapse. They may take out electric, gas, and telephone lines, disrupting service for days, weeks, or months. Some quakes are powerful enough to set off flash floods, land-slides, fires, and even tsunamis. In many instances, these side effects of the ground shaking produce more structural damage, injuries, and deaths than the earthquake itself.

Earthquake Possibilities

Should you be concerned about the possibility of an earth-quake in your area? If you don't live in California, you might think that there is no reason for concern. You might be sur-prised to learn, however, that earthquakes can occur in all fifty states and U.S. territories. Forty-five states are at moder-ate to high risk. Only five states are at low risk—Florida,

Pakistanis walk through the ruins of buildings that were destroyed by an earthquake in Pakistan-administered Kashmir in October 2005. The earthquake killed more than 50,000 people, injured tens of thousands, and left millions homeless. Seismologists don't know exactly when and where an earthquake will occur next, but they do know where they have struck previously and understand that earthquakes will hit the same area again.

North Dakota, Minnesota, Wisconsin, and Michigan. Although regions west of the Rocky Mountains experience earthquakes more often than other areas, the central United States has experienced the most violent earthquakes.

Scientists do not know when or where an earthquake will strike next. They do know, however, that where earthquakes have struck before, they will strike again. What does this information mean to you? No matter where you live, it is possible that you will experience an earthquake someday. In May 2005, the U.S. Geological Survey (USGS) announced to the public that it had begun to publish statistical probabilities of a moderate earthquake striking

Earthquake Country

If someone asked you to name the state that has had the largest number of earthquakes, would you say California? Although that is the answer most people probably would give, it's actually incorrect. California has had the most damaging earthquakes, but Alaska is the state that has had the greatest number of earthquakes. In fact, Alaska accounts for more than half of all earthquakes in the United States. Most of these occur in uninhabited areas, so the damage is minimal. According to the U.S. Geological Survey, the top ten earthquake states from 1974 to 2003 are:

Alaska

California

Hawaii

Nevada

Washington

Idaho

Wyoming

Montana

Utah

Oregon

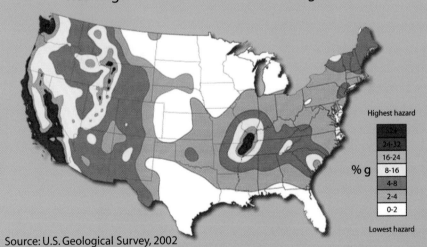

Highest hazard

%g

| 32+ |
| 24-32 |
| 16-24 |
| 8-16 |
| 4-8 |
| 2-4 |
| 0-2 |

Lowest hazard

Source: U.S. Geological Survey, 2002

The National Seismic Hazard Mapping Project of the USGS (http://earthquake. usgs.gov/hazmaps) provides maps showing data about faults and earthquake hazards in the United States, including Alaska and Hawaii. This map shows the highest and lowest hazards in the forty-eight conterminous states in 2002.

California over a twenty-four-hour period. The forecasts do not provide warnings or predictions of imminent major quakes but instead display the chances and distribution of aftershocks from earthquakes that have already hit. The forecasting models are found at the USGS Web site at http://pasadena.wr.usgs.gov/step. What's the best way to protect yourself, your family members, and your home? Be prepared! Read on to learn more.

Measuring Earthquakes

Scientists find out the strength and location of earthquakes by using a recording device called a seismograph. These

A seismologist holds up the seismograph printout at an earthquake-monitoring station on January 25, 2005, in Aceh Besar, Indonesia. The magnitude 9.15 earthquake made the seismograph's needle fluctuate so wildly that it ripped holes in and splattered ink on the graph paper.

🌏 Earthquake Scientists 🌏

You have learned about two scales for measuring earthquakes—the Richter scale and the Modified Mercalli scale—but do you know how they were named? The Richter scale is named after Charles F. Richter (1900–1985), the American physicist and seismologist who developed it. Born in Ohio, Richter moved to Los Angeles in 1916. After earning a doctorate degree at the California Institute of Technology (Caltech), he taught physics and seismology there. In 1935, Richter worked with Beno Gutenberg (1889–1960), another Caltech professor, to develop the scale for measuring the magnitude of earthquakes.

The Richter scale replaced the older Mercalli scale, which had been originally developed by Giuseppe Mercalli (1850–1914) in 1902. Mercalli was an Italian scientist. In 1931, the original Mercalli scale was modified into its current version, which provides a more accurate measurement of an earthquake's intensity.

scientists, known as seismologists, measure ground movements in three different directions—east-west, north-south, and up-down. Some seismographs are so sensitive that they can detect even the smallest ground motions. They can detect these motions from both close and faraway earthquakes.

Earthquakes are most commonly measured by two scales—the Richter scale and the Modified Mercalli scale. The Richter scale is the more well known of the two. It measures the amount of energy an earthquake releases and records it as a "magnitude." The 1989 Loma Prieta,

California, earthquake, for example, had a magnitude of 7.1. For every increase of one whole number on the Richter scale, the amount of energy released by the earthquake is thirty-two times greater. That means that a magnitude 8.0

EARTHQUAKE SCALES

Richter Scale	Level of Damage	Modified Mercalli Scale
4.3 or less	No damage.	I – IV Instrumental to Moderate
4.4 – 4.8	Very minor damage. Some glassware and dishes broken; small objects moved.	V Rather Strong
4.9 – 5.4	Minor damage. Glassware, dishes, and windows broken; furniture moved or knocked over.	VI Strong
5.5 – 6.1	Moderate damage to well-constructed buildings; significant damage to poorly constructed buildings.	VII Very Strong
6.2 – 6.5	Significant structural damage. Chimneys and towers may fall; damage to trees; frame houses may move.	VIII Destructive
6.6 – 6.9	Severe structural damage, including collapse of some buildings. Damage to foundations; broken underground pipes; ground cracks; liquefaction.	IX Ruinous
7.0 – 7.3	Destruction of most frame and masonry structures and foundations; some bridges destroyed.	X Disastrous
7.4 – 8.1	Nearly all masonry structures and bridges destroyed; wide cracks in ground; extensive landslides.	XI Very Disastrous
Higher than 8.1	Nearly complete destruction; large rock masses shifted.	XII Catastrophic

Source: FEMA for Kids

earthquake releases thirty-two times more energy than a magnitude 7.0 quake.

The Modified Mercalli scale measures intensity based on the effects of an earthquake. The ratings are determined by direct observations of the damage caused by the quake at specific locations. Because the effects of one earthquake can vary greatly from one location to another, there may be a range of intensity values. The Modified Mercalli scale presents measurements in Roman numerals, ranging from I (on the low end) to XII (on the high end). The Loma Prieta earthquake was rated as high as XI on the Modified Mercalli scale.

2 --- Preparing for Earthquakes

Why is it so important to be prepared for an earthquake? As you have learned, earthquakes strike without warning. In the aftermath of a quake, utility lines are often broken. When this happens, electricity, gas, water, and telephone services may be unavailable for hours, days, or even weeks. Would you be able to cope? By preparing ahead of time, you will have the supplies you need when you need them. Being prepared will also help you feel calmer and less stressed if an earthquake does strike.

Making a Disaster Plan

A disaster plan is a plan of action that you put together with your family. It helps all family members know what they need to do in the event of a disaster. Having a disaster plan is also a good way to make sure that family members find one another if they become separated. The following tips are useful when creating a disaster plan for earthquakes:

- For every room of your home, select a spot where you would be safe during an earthquake. Choose a place where you would be protected from falling objects. The safest locations include underneath a sturdy desk or table, or against a wall inside the house.

These first-graders at a public school in Oregon participate in an earthquake drill in 2002 by finding protection beneath tables and chairs. Nine years earlier, an earthquake destroyed the school. Today Oregon legislators work to make new schools, law enforcement agency buildings, and fire stations earthquake resistant.

- Select two relatives or friends who do not live in your area—one to be the primary contact and one to be the alternate contact. Make sure that all family members know the contacts' phone numbers. In the event of an earthquake, everyone can contact that person so that all family members' whereabouts are known.

- Make sure that every adult family member knows how to use a fire extinguisher. Training can be obtained from the local fire department.

- Get training in first aid. Check with your local American Red Cross chapter to see if it offers first-aid classes.

EARTHQUAKE SUPPLIES CHECKLIST

Food and Beverages

✓ Canned meats, canned fruits and vegetables, and canned or instant soup.

✓ Cereals, such as granola and oatmeal.

✓ Nutritious snacks, such as granola bars, trail mix, and raisins.

✓ Bottled water, juice boxes, or foil packets.

✓ Food for babies or family members with special dietary needs.

✓ Dry or canned food for pets.

Equipment

✓ First-aid kit.

✓ Flashlight with extra batteries.

✓ Portable radio or television (battery operated).

✓ Manual can opener.

✓ Cell-phone charger, preferably one with an adapter that can be plugged into a car's lighter for using the car's battery, in case there is a power outage. (Do not keep your cell phone in your supply kit, though.)

Personal Items

✓ Money (in small bills).

✓ Copies of personal identification.

✓ Medications.

✓ Change of clothing, including shoes, for each family member.

✓ Blanket or sleeping bag for each family member.

✓ Personal hygiene items, including toilet tissue, soap, shampoo, toothbrush and toothpaste, comb and brush.

✓ A whistle for use in calling for assistance.

Disaster Supplies Kit

An essential part of your family's disaster plan is a disaster supplies kit. This kit contains basic items that family members would likely need in the event of a disaster such as an earthquake. These items should be kept near the door to your home and stored in a portable container. The best types of containers are sturdy and easy to carry, such as backpacks, duffel bags, and covered plastic trash cans. Your kit should contain at least a three-day supply of water and nonperishable foods.

Be certain to store foods in a cool, dry place, and make sure that food containers are closed tightly. Rotate your

A customer care representative in an American Red Cross store in San Francisco, California, unpacked a two-person emergency preparedness kit in June 2005. Every family should make a disaster supply kit available in the home to use in any emergency, such as an earthquake, hurricane, flood, wildfire, or tornado.

food supply periodically. Use foods that are nearing their expiration date, and replace them with new supplies. A well-stocked disaster supplies kit will help your family be prepared if an earthquake does strike—whether you stay sheltered at home or are forced to evacuate.

Safe Drinking Water

What could possibly be even more important for survival than food? Water. Most people could survive for about a month without food. The same cannot be said for surviving without water. After only a week, dehydration begins to take its toll and can quickly turn into a life-threatening emergency. For this reason, it is extremely important to

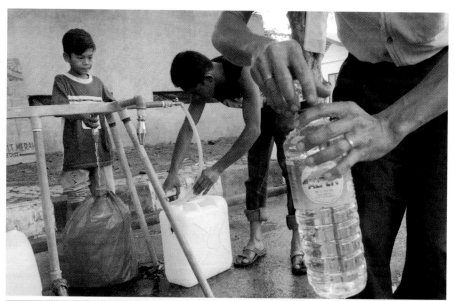

In Banda Aceh, Indonesia, people filled jugs with purified water three months after the devastating December 2004 earthquake and tsunami. The ten-year-old student pictured here said that he and his family had no other source of drinking water, so every day before school he came to this water supply station.

stock safe drinking water in your home. If an earthquake were to strike, water or sewage lines could be broken. Public water supplies, then, might not be available or might be contaminated. In this case, you would need to rely on your personal supplies of water for survival.

How much water will you need? At minimum, store a three-day supply of water for each family member. Some experts recommend storing a two-week supply per family member, if possible. Water needs differ from person to person, depending on such factors as age, activity level, and climate. As a general rule of thumb, though, store 1 gallon (3.8 liters) of water per person, per day.

Storing Water

The best way to store water is to put it in clean plastic or glass containers. Two-liter plastic soft-drink bottles are a good choice. It is not safe to use any container that has ever held toxic substances. To prevent the growth of microorganisms, treat the water with chlorine bleach before storing it. For each quart of water, add two drops of liquid chlorine bleach (containing 5.25 percent sodium hypochlorite [chlorine]), and stir it into the water. Then close the water containers tightly, label them with the date, and put them in a cool, dark place for storage. Replace the water every six months to ensure freshness.

Hidden Water Sources

What could you do if an earthquake caught you off guard without a supply of clean water? Your home has a few hidden sources of water that you can use in an emergency. The freezer probably contains ice cubes, which you can melt and drink. The hot water tank also contains a supply of water. Before accessing the water in this tank, make sure that an adult has turned off the gas or electricity. If you have run out of other options, the water in the reservoir tank (not the bowl) of the toilet may be used. This water must be purified first, however.

Purifying Water

In an emergency, you might be able to use water from outdoor sources. Choose rainwater, ponds and lakes, streams and rivers, and natural springs. However, be sure to purify this water before you drink it. The Federal Emergency Management Agency (FEMA) recommends three simple ways to purify water:

1. **Boiling.** This is the safest way to purify water. Bring water to a rolling boil, and continue boiling for ten minutes. Allow water to cool before drinking.

2. **Chlorination.** With this method, liquid chlorine bleach is used to kill microorganisms. With an eyedropper, add two drops of bleach to 1 quart (1 l) of water. Stir the water and let it stand for thirty minutes.

3. **Purification Tablets.** These tablets, which release chlorine or iodine, can be purchased at sporting goods stores or drugstores. Follow the directions on the package.

Safeguarding Your Home

In addition to preparing yourself for an earthquake, you also need to prepare your home. There are actions you can

FIRST-AID KIT

✔ First-aid manual

✔ Sterile adhesive bandages (assorted sizes)

✔ Sterile gauze pads (2-inch and 4-inch [5.1- and 10.2-centimeter] sizes)

✔ Sterile roll bandages (2-inch and 3-inch [5.1- and 7.6-cm] sizes)

✔ Adhesive tape

✔ Soap

✔ Antibiotic ointment

✔ Petroleum jelly

✔ Sunscreen

✔ Scissors

✔ Tweezers

✔ Sewing needle

✔ Safety pins

✔ Moistened towelettes

✔ Latex gloves

✔ Thermometer

✔ Nonprescription medications including aspirin or nonaspirin pain reliever, antacid, antidiarrheal medication

take to help protect your home and your valuables from damage. To safeguard your home from an earthquake, work with family members to:

- Install latches on drawers and cabinet doors. Doing so will prevent the drawers and cabinet doors from accidentally opening during an earthquake and spilling their contents.

- Bolt or strap tall bookcases, filing cabinets, and cupboards to the wall. Store heavy items on the bottom shelves. These actions will help reduce the risk of damage, as well as injury from falling objects.

- Make sure that your water heater is strapped to the wall. If it is not, encourage adult family members to have this done. A gas water heater that topples over in an earthquake could break the gas line, igniting a fire.

- Find out if your home is connected to the foundation with bolts. Having inexpensive anchor bolts installed around the outside of your home can help prevent damage from an earthquake.

Tips for People Who Have Disabilities

For those people with special needs, a natural disaster can be an especially scary event. People who have disabilities may feel particularly vulnerable during an earthquake. With careful preparation, however, the experience will most likely seem more manageable and less frightening. People

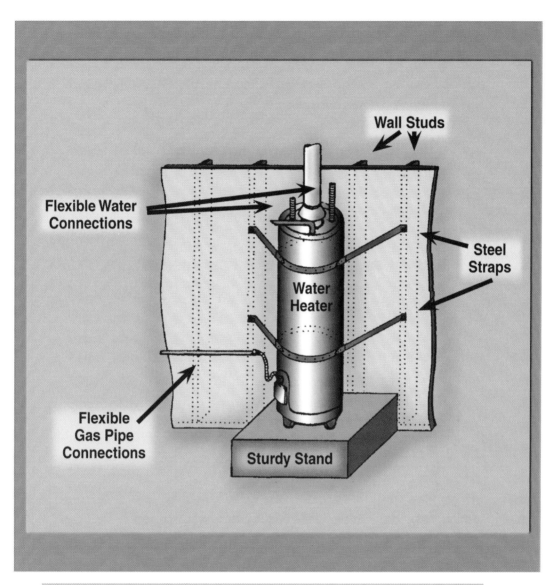

Flexible Water Connections

Wall Studs

Steel Straps

Water Heater

Flexible Gas Pipe Connections

Sturdy Stand

This illustration shows how to secure a hot water heater to wall studs by using steel straps. By strapping a water heater and having it fitted with a flexible gas supply line, your family will reduce the risk of a fire or explosion from a gas leak during or after an earthquake. It is best to make sure that you strap the heater at least 4 inches (10.2 cm) above the water controls and about one-third of the way down from the top of the heater. If the water heater sits on a stand, make sure someone secures the stand to the wall or floor so that it will not move out from under the heater during an earthquake.

with special needs have to safeguard their home, create a disaster plan, and assemble a disaster kit also. Here are some additional tips to help those with special needs prepare for an earthquake:

- Set up a buddy system with family members, friends, or neighbors.

- Make a list of important names, addresses, and phone numbers, such as those of doctors, pharmacies, family members, and friends. Also list any medications, allergies, or special needs. Keep a copy of the list, and give a copy to your buddy.

- If you have a visual impairment, be sure to keep an extra pair of eyeglasses, contacts and contact solution, and a few extra canes in different places around your home. It would also be wise to plan several evacuation routes from your home.

- If you have a hearing impairment, be sure to keep a battery-operated television and extra batteries as part of your earthquake supplies. A pen and paper for communicating are also essential supplies.

- If you use a wheelchair, you may want to keep medications, a small flashlight, and a whistle in a small bag attached to your wheelchair. The whistle can be used to alert others to your location in the event of an earthquake.

Don't Forget Fluffy

When preparing your family disaster plan, be sure to consider your dogs, cats, and other pets. An important part of planning ahead involves having identification on dogs and cats at all times. This way, if your pet gets loose in the confusion of an earthquake, he or she could be returned to you. Collars with identification tags should include your name, address, and phone number. In addition to identification, make sure that your pet's required vaccinations are up-to-date.

If you need to evacuate during an earthquake, you will need to make arrangements for your animals, too. It is safest for your pets for you to take them with you. Leaving pets behind puts them in danger. Keep in mind, however, that most emergency shelters will not take animals due to public health and safety concerns. One exception is trained dog guides for people who have disabilities. You may want to check with motels outside your local area to find out which ones accept pets in emergency situations. Local boarding kennels may be another option when evacuating pets. Most will require proof of current vaccinations. Make a list of "pet-friendly" places, and keep the list in your earthquake supplies kit.

If you take pets with you, remember to follow these tips:

- Have a portable carrier available to transport cats and small, or medium-sized dogs. Put large dogs on a leash.

- Be sure that dogs and cats are wearing collars with identification tags.

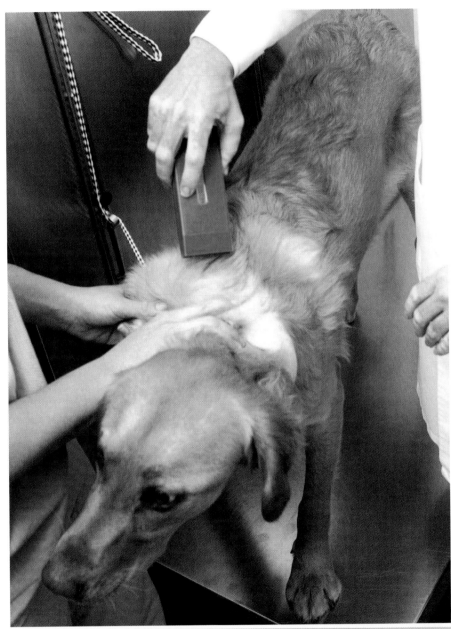

A veterinarian uses a handheld scanner to read this yellow Labrador retriever's identification number. Many people are having microchips implanted in their pets to make identifying them easier than a collar ID tag when the animals are lost or stolen. Make sure, though, that your dog, cat, or other pet wears an identification tag at all times in case you become separated from the pet during an emergency.

- Bring pet food, bottled water, and bowls for food and water. Bring litter and a litter box for cats.

- If your pet needs medication, be sure to take it with you; keep your pet's health and vaccination records handy.

If you must leave pets behind, then abide by these guidelines:

- Put your pets in a safe interior room with good airflow, such as a bathroom. Do not confine cats and dogs to the same room. Make sure that birds, hamsters, and other small pets remain in secure cages.

- Be sure that dogs and cats are wearing collars with identification tags.

- Arrange the pet's usual bedding, and leave favorite toys. Provide a litter box with fresh litter for cats.

- Provide a three-day supply of food and water. A good solution may be to use a self-feeder and automatic water dispenser.

- Write a note informing others of your pet's location within the home and attach it to the front door. Include a telephone number where you can be reached.

- Never leave pets outside during an evacuation.

Creating a disaster plan and supplies kit, and safeguarding your home will help you be prepared in the event of an earthquake. An essential part of earthquake preparedness, however, involves knowing what will happen when the ground begins to shake, and learning what you can do to stay safe.

3 --- On Shaky Ground

You are at home eating breakfast, preparing for school. As you eat a bowl of cereal, you suddenly notice that the juice in your glass is rocking back and forth, as if someone has just nudged the glass. Then you begin to feel the vibrations. The lamp above your head begins to sway, and the box of cereal on the table in front of you falls over. The vibrations increase quickly. You suddenly think to yourself, it's an earthquake! What do you do now?

Why is it so important to be prepared and to know what to do if an earthquake hits? Most earthquakes last only a few seconds, but it can seem like a long time when you actually experience one. As we have already seen, planning for an earthquake decreases your chances of getting injured when one actually occurs. However, you also need to know what to expect and how to react during an actual earthquake.

First Response

During an earthquake, the actual movement of the ground generally does not cause the most injuries and damages. The majority of injuries are caused by falling objects, flying glass, and walls caving in. By being prepared, knowing what to expect, and practicing your response, you can prevent most earthquake-related injuries and help keep yourself and your family members safe.

In the past, experts recommended finding the nearest doorway to stand in when an earthquake hits. The reasoning was that doorways are more stable than the rest of a room and are less likely to collapse. Today, we know that this is simply not true. Standing in a doorway leaves you vulnerable to falling debris and collapsing structures. Hiding under a table or similar shelter will help protect you from falling bookcases, dishes, walls, etc. Despite the modern advice regarding earthquake safety, many people still run for the nearest doorway when an earthquake strikes, resulting in more, rather than fewer, injuries. Let's discuss the best methods for staying safe during an earthquake.

QUAKE MYTHS AND FACTS

Myth: Earthquakes are most likely to occur in early morning.

Fact: Earthquakes don't follow any pattern. They are just as likely to strike during the afternoon or evening as they are in the morning.

Myth: Earthquakes occur most often in certain types of weather, such as during hot and dry conditions.

Fact: There is no such thing as "earthquake weather." Earthquakes can occur at any time of year. They are just as likely to strike in winter as in summer, in rainy weather as in dry weather.

Myth: Earthquakes cause both tsunamis and tidal waves.

Fact: Although tsunamis and tidal waves are both large sea waves, they are different. A tsunami is a sea wave produced by an underwater earthquake. A tidal wave is a sea wave caused by high winds.

Myth: Scientists can predict when earthquakes will occur.

Fact: Earthquakes cannot be predicted or prevented, but being prepared will help you stay safe.

Sources: U.S. Geological Survey; FEMA for Kids

Drop, Cover, and Hold!

During an earthquake, you can stay as safe as possible by following three simple steps. Just remember to drop, cover, and hold. The Federal Emergency Management Agency (FEMA), the American Red Cross, and the Centers for Disease Control and Prevention (CDC) recommend these steps:

- Drop to the ground. You are safer on the ground, where you can't lose your balance and fall while the earth is shaking.

- Take cover. If possible, get underneath a table, desk, or other sturdy piece of furniture. Cover your face with your arm to protect your eyes from flying glass or other sharp objects. If you are in bed, stay there and protect your head with your pillow.

- Hold. If you are under a desk or table, hold on to a leg of the furniture with your free arm. Stay where you are until the shaking stops. Trying to move to a different location during an earthquake could result in serious injury.

Think About Where You Are

The best way to act during an earthquake depends on your location.

If You Are Inside

If the ground begins to shake and you are inside your home, school, or other building, stay inside. You are safer indoors than outdoors. Trying to leave a building during an

As a partner in the National Earthquake Hazards Reduction Program, the Federal Emergency Management Agency (FEMA) advises to drop, cover, and hold during an earthquake. This means that you should drop to the ground, take cover beneath furniture, such as a sturdy table, and hold on until the shaking has stopped. If you cannot seek cover under a table, make sure you have crouched to the ground and clasp your hands over your head for protection.

earthquake is dangerous because you're more likely to be injured by falling objects and flying debris. Instead, follow the "drop, cover, and hold" steps to protect yourself and stay safe. Be sure to keep away from windows because the glass may shatter. Also, stay clear of bookcases or other tall furniture that might topple over in a quake. If possible, move toward an inner wall or hallway until the shaking is over.

If you are in an apartment building or other public structure, such as an office building, be prepared for fire alarms and overhead sprinklers to turn on during or just after the quake. Do not get in an elevator during or after an earthquake. Know the best routes for escape in any public building.

Public places such as movie theaters, auditoriums, sports arenas, and gyms often do not have sturdy furniture under which you can find shelter. They are also often crowded. If you are in one of these public places when an earthquake occurs, stay as calm as you can, get low to the ground, and cover your head and face with your arms. If you are in a seat, stay in it or crawl under it if possible. If you are with younger kids, help them to do the same. Avoid hallways or aisles where others may try to run for the exits or a doorway to stand in. Again, expect fire alarms and sprinklers to activate, and never get in an elevator.

If You Are in an Elevator

If you are in an elevator when an earthquake occurs, get low to the ground and stay calm. Elevators are made to lock in place during an emergency such as an earthquake, so you do not have to worry about falling. Neither do you have to worry about things falling on you. However, you may be

Movie theaters or auditoriums such as the one pictured here can become crowded and might not have sturdy furniture under which you may find protection during an earthquake. However, if you are in a public place when a quake hits, try to remain calm, stay clear of the aisles, and get low to the ground. Cover your head and face with your arms.

stuck in the elevator until the electricity is restored or until you are rescued by the police or fire department. Most elevators have a telephone or intercom that allows you to inform an operator that you are trapped. The operator will tell you when you can expect to be rescued. Above all, remain calm and don't panic. Someone will rescue you, even though it may take some time.

If You Are Outdoors

If you feel the ground begin to shake when you are outdoors, the safest course of action is to move to an open area. Keep clear of buildings, utility poles, streetlights, overpasses, trees, and any other objects that may fall on you.

Residents of Lima, Peru, participated in an earthquake drill on October 11, 1999. For ten minutes, the entire country took part in the drill, which was designed to familiarize citizens with earthquake emergency procedures. Having a clear plan of action and practicing it will help you, your family, and your friends be prepared for a natural disaster when one occurs.

After you have reached an open area, drop down to the ground. Stay there until the tremors have stopped.

If You Are in a Vehicle

If you are traveling in a vehicle when an earthquake occurs, stop the vehicle as quickly as possible and remain inside. Try to stop in an open area that is away from buildings, utility poles, streetlights, and trees. After the earth has stopped shaking, proceed with extreme caution. Always make sure there is road ahead to drive on. Avoid traveling on highway ramps or bridges that may have suffered damage in the earthquake. If the conditions ahead appear too hazardous to attempt—perhaps from downed electrical lines, debris in the road, injuries, etc.—find a safe place to park and wait.

Transamerica Pyramid

San Francisco, California, is located in an active earthquake region. In this area, it is important for tall buildings to be designed with tremors in mind. San Francisco's tallest building and one of its most famous landmarks was specially engineered to withstand earthquakes. The Transamerica Pyramid, completed in 1972, is a forty-eight-story-high office building in San Francisco. Its unique pyramid shape gives the structure more stability than a typical skyscraper. In addition, the 853-foot-high (260 m) pyramid is built on a steel-and-concrete foundation buried 52 feet (16 m) in the ground and designed to move with tremors. During the 1989 Loma Prieta earthquake, the pyramid shook for more than a minute and the top story swayed nearly a foot (0.3 m). Even so, the Transamerica Pyramid was undamaged.

San Francisco's Transamerica Pyramid, on Columbus Street, is located in an active earthquake area. The construction of this building was completed in 1972. The architects and engineers designed the structure with earthquake-resistant technologies of that time. The building sustained no damage during a 1989 quake.

Protecting Your Pets

Much like small children, pets are especially vulnerable during disasters such as earthquakes. Animals don't understand what is going on around them and may become scared and agitated. During an earthquake, bring your pets inside as soon as possible. It is dangerous for them to be outdoors, and they may be more likely to run away if they are afraid. Once they are safely inside, keep cats and dogs separated. The anxiety they feel during an earthquake may cause some cats and dogs to act strangely—even those that usually get along with one another. If you need to evacuate after an earthquake, follow your disaster plan and take pets with you if at all possible.

Don't Panic

The most important thing to remember during an earthquake is to stay calm. Panic is one of the leading causes of injury during and after an earthquake. Panic can cause you to forget the things for which you are prepared. People who lose control may try to run away or leave a building instead of finding a safe place to drop, cover, and hold on. When adults and teenagers panic, small children are also more likely to be frightened.

To avoid panicking during an actual earthquake, practice the steps you would take beforehand. Know exactly what you will do if an earthquake ever strikes. Being prepared will help you to stay in control, keeping you and others around you as safe as possible. Frequently repeating your plan of action will allow you to be better prepared to deal with the aftermath of an earthquake.

4 --- In the Wake of a Quake

Earthquakes cause the ground to shake uncontrollably. This shaking is the cause of most of the damage attributed to an earthquake. Depending on the magnitude of the shaking, you can expect to see several types of damage. Shaking can cause buildings and bridges to crack or even collapse. Power lines and telephone poles may have been knocked over. Windows may have shattered and fallen to the ground or street below. You may even see a fault line that has reached the surface, leaving a dangerous crack or hole in the ground. Inside, furniture and decorations may have fallen to the floor, and walls may have become cracked.

The extent of these damages depends on the amount of shaking produced by the earthquake. The closer you are to the source of the earthquake, the more violent the shaking will be. Damage can also occur because of liquefaction. Liquefaction occurs where the soil is loose, sandy, or contains more water than most soil. This loose soil shakes so much during an earthquake that it can temporarily act like water. Buildings constructed atop loose or water-saturated soil can become very unstable during an earthquake. These structures are more likely to collapse or fall over compared to buildings constructed on more solid ground.

Many earthquakes are followed by a series of (usually) smaller earthquakes known as aftershocks, which can

After the January 2004 San Simeon earthquake in California, this home separated from its foundation. Aftershocks from an earthquake can cause additional damage because structures have already been weakened by the original quake. Make sure you do not occupy unsafe buildings, and remember to have your family members photograph damage to your home for any insurance claims that might need to be filed afterward.

cause significant additional damage and harm. Aftershocks often result in great damage because the original earthquake has already weakened structures, making them less sturdy and safe. Aftershocks often cause previously damaged structures to experience more damage and sometimes to fall down altogether.

There are several secondary hazards that often occur after an earthquake that can cause an amount of damage similar to the actual earthquake itself. Many earthquakes are followed by fires due to ruptured gas lines and fallen electrical cables. Floods may result from broken or cracked water lines, dams, and levees. Landslides and mudslides can occur on hillsides, mountainsides, and riverbanks where an earthquake has loosened the soil. Strong landslides have been known to bury hundreds of homes and hundreds of people. A tsunami is a series of giant waves caused by an underwater earthquake or an undersea volcanic eruption. These giant waves can inflict great damage to coastline properties. Sometimes hazardous materials may be released into the environment due to an earthquake. Downed lines of communication often delays the emergency response to secondary hazards, increasing the damage caused by them.

What to Do

After the earth stops shaking, the first thing you need to do is make sure that you are all right. Check yourself for cuts, bruises, and other injuries. After an earthquake, if you are alone, trapped, or injured, stay as calm as you can and yell for help. Other people may not know that you need help unless you yell to let them know. Yelling will help to draw attention to you. Before moving around, put on sturdy shoes. There may be shards of glass on the floor, so it's best not to walk around barefoot. If possible, dress in long pants and a long-sleeved shirt and wear work gloves. Dressing in this manner will help you stay protected from additional dangers.

After taking care of yourself, check those around you. Look for injuries or other earthquake-related problems, such as someone who might be trapped under debris. Be especially mindful of others who may not be able to help themselves, including small children, elderly people, people who have disabilities, and pets. Give first aid to anyone who is injured. If the injuries are very serious, call 911 or your local emergency number. Keep in mind, though, that telephone service may not be available immediately following an earthquake. Be sure to use the telephone only to report life-threatening emergencies.

When you are sure that everyone is safe, inspect the building for damage. The X-shaped cracks in walls are often a sign of greater damage. It may indicate that the entire wall has shifted and is unstable, and you should leave the building immediately. Any small fires should be put out with a fire extinguisher. If you smell gas, inform an adult. He or she should turn off the gas if there is a leak and get out

Helping Pets

Immediately following an earthquake, you may have trouble locating your pets. When animals are frightened, they often try to isolate themselves. A dog may find a hiding place under a bed or in a dark corner. A cat may seek safety under a couch or in a bathtub. Although pets usually come out of hiding on their own, they may need a little coaxing.

In the days following an earthquake, be especially attentive to pets. When taking a dog outside, be sure to use a leash. Outdoor conditions may have changed during the earthquake, and dogs may become disoriented and try to run away. Be on the lookout for downed power lines, which are hazardous to both animals and humans. Some pets are particularly sensitive to environmental changes, and they may show behavioral problems after an earthquake. For example, a dog that is usually friendly may suddenly become aggressive. Keep a close eye on pets until conditions have returned to normal.

of the house. (Do not light matches.) If the building you are in seems unsafe, make sure that everyone gets out. Don't drink the water until you are sure that it's safe. Listen to the radio for instructions from community leaders.

What If There Is a Fire?

Fires are one of the most frequent and hazardous results of earthquakes. Quakes can knock down power lines and break gas lines, both of which can result in large, dangerous fires. Inside, earthquakes can knock over water heaters, large appliances, lamps, and candles. All of these things could start a fire in your home. Water pipes are often broken during an earthquake, which can make fighting a fire difficult or impossible.

After a severe earthquake hit Southern California in January 1994, a resident of a trailer park reacted to a fire that set a neighbor's home ablaze. Earthquakes cause gas and power lines to rupture and can lead to deadly fires.

After an earthquake, quickly put out any small fires if it is safe to do so. Never use water to put out electrical fires. If a loss of power has left you in the dark, use flashlights instead of candles. Candles could fall over and start a fire during an aftershock, and they could cause a gas leak to explode. If you smell gas, quickly shut off the gas at the meter.

Use a first-aid kit to treat minor burns immediately. Call 911 or your local emergency number to report serious burns, but remember that phone lines may be down or overloaded just after an earthquake. If possible, wait fifteen to thirty minutes to use the phone. However, if a fire threatens to get out of control, get away from it and contact 911 or your emergency services immediately.

What If You Lose Electricity?

Loss of electricity and phone service is a common occurrence following an earthquake. Carefully inspect the inside and outside of your home to make sure there are no broken electrical lines. Stay away from downed power lines, and call 911 or your local emergency number immediately to report them. Turn off lights and appliances that were on when the blackout occurred. Keep your refrigerator and freezer shut for as long as possible to keep food from spoiling. You should prepare for a loss of electricity by keeping several flashlights handy with charged batteries.

Coping with an Earthquake

Experiencing an earthquake can be dangerous and scary. There are several things to remember that will help you

Indonesian Tsunami (2004)

On December 26, 2004, an earthquake in the Indian Ocean near the island of Sumatra, Indonesia, measured 9.15 on the Richter scale, making it one of the largest earthquakes on Earth in the last forty years. Just one hour after the earthquake hit, seismometers that monitored Mount Wrangell in Alaska recorded fourteen smaller earthquakes within eleven minutes. The earthquake, which started about 180 miles (290 km) south of Banda Aceh, the city on Sumatra hardest hit by the disaster, triggered a tsunami that caused a historic amount of destruction. The earthquake, tsunami, and resulting floods caused about 300,000 deaths (although the exact number of deaths may never be known). In addition, enormous property damages left about 1 million people homeless.

The Indonesian earthquake of 2004 was so powerful that it caused Earth's rotation to speed up; every day is now 2.68 microseconds (0.00000268 second) quicker. The North Pole is now about 1 inch (25 cm) east of its previous position. The tsunami created by the earthquake was strong enough to permanently alter the coastlines of several Southeast Asian countries. Many ecosystems in the wake of the tsunami were changed or completely destroyed.

Since this natural disaster took place, countries all over the world have contributed money, supplies, and man power to the nations that were hit hardest by the earthquake and tsunami. A global effort has been enacted to help create an early warning system in the Indian Ocean in hopes of reducing the loss of life and property should a similar tsunami ever strike this area of the world again.

On December 30, 2004, these volunteers and residents of Nagappattinam, India, fled their town when an alarm signaled that a tsunami was about to hit. Although it was a false alarm, aftershocks in the Indian Ocean caused many people to panic. When you believe a tsunami is close to striking, always seek higher ground inland.

cope with the consequences of an earthquake. Remember that the actual earthquake itself will only last for a little while, and that it will be over soon. It may take some time for you to return to your normal routine, so make the best of your situation. Don't keep your emotions inside if you are afraid or confused. Tell your parents or other adults how you feel, and don't be afraid to ask questions. Helping others is another way of coping. Lastly, remember that even though an earthquake can be scary, and the aftermath can be difficult to deal with, things will get better.

Reducing the Damage

Earthquakes are the most powerful, destructive, and unpredictable of all natural disasters. The power of Earth's immense plates grinding together is a force unparalleled anywhere else on this planet, and there is very little—if anything—that humans can do to contain that power. This does not mean, however, that we can't reduce the disastrous effects of nature's most destructive force.

FEMA has disaster field offices, such as this one in California. The employees pictured here were trying to deal with the recovery efforts after the Northridge earthquake in 1994. FEMA helps the National Earthquakes Hazards Reduction Program (NEHRP) to minimize the damage caused by earthquakes in many ways, including educating the public about post-earthquake damage.

In 1977, Congress established the National Earthquakes Hazards Reduction Program (NEHRP) to help reduce the risks to life and property due to earthquakes in the United States. NEHRP is a combination of the efforts of four groups to improve our knowledge and reaction to earthquakes. These groups include the Federal Emergency Management Agency (FEMA), the National Institutes of Standards and Technology (NIST), the National Science Foundation (NSF), and the United States Geological Survey (USGS). This program has helped to minimize the damage caused by earthquakes by assessing and fixing potentially hazardous situations, improving building codes and land-use policies, and studying post-earthquake damage to improve education about this unpredictable natural force. The NEHRP seeks to evaluate the risks involved with earthquakes and to reduce those risks as much as possible.

These structural engineers met outside the quake-damaged Los Angeles Memorial Coliseum in 1994 to assess damage from the Northridge earthquake. FEMA distributes grants to help in rebuilding efforts after earthquakes, fires, floods, and other natural disasters.

A FEMA inspector examines a home that was damaged during a Seattle, Washington, earthquake in 2001. Homeowners should be knowledgeable about insurance policies for earthquake claims and photograph all damage that was caused during the disaster. In addition, they should keep all receipts for any expenses that they incur if they have to evacuate their homes.

The NEHRP encompasses four main goals:

1. Develop effective practices and policies for earthquake loss-reduction and accelerate their implementation;

2. Improve techniques to reduce seismic vulnerability of facilities and systems;

3. Improve seismic hazards identification and risk-assessment methods and their use;

4. Improve the understanding of earthquakes and their effects.

Thanks to the NEHRP, the United States has been able to reduce the deaths, injuries, and damages that result from earthquakes and their aftershocks. Knowledge and thoughtful planning have been our two most effective weapons against earthquakes. In this book, we have discussed the facts about earthquakes and earthquake safety to better prepare you in case one should hit where you live. By remaining calm and remembering these tips, you can survive an earthquake and help others to do the same.

Glossary

aftershock A less powerful earthquake that comes after a large earthquake.

conterminous Contained in the same boundaries, as in the forty-eight states of the United States. Alaska and Hawaii are not conterminous states.

dehydration An abnormal loss of water or body fluids.

epicenter The point on Earth's surface where an earthquake begins, located directly above the focus.

evacuate To leave an area because of dangerous circumstances.

fault A crack in Earth's crust where large rock plates slide past one another.

focus The point along a fault where rock plates first break apart, causing the start of an earthquake.

intensity The measurement of the effect of something, such as an earthquake's effects.

liquefaction The changing of loose soil into a fluidlike substance caused by the shaking of an earthquake.

magnitude A number used to measure the power and strength of an earthquake.

Modified Mercalli scale A scale used to measure the intensity of an earthquake.

nonperishable Not likely to spoil.

plate tectonics A scientific theory involving the movement of large rock plates within the earth used to explain the occurrence of earthquakes.

Richter scale A scale used to measure the magnitude of an earthquake.

seismograph A device used to record ground movements.

tremor The ground shaking caused by an earthquake.

tsunami A shoreward-bound series of huge waves caused by an underwater earthquake, an undersea volcanic eruption, or an undersea landslide.

For More Information

American Red Cross
National Headquarters
2025 E Street NW
Washington, DC 20006
(202) 303-4498
Web site: http://www.redcross.org

Canadian Center for Emergency Preparedness
77 James Street North, Suite 325
Hamilton, ON L8R2K3
Canada
(905) 331-2552
Web site: http://www.ccep.ca

DisasterHelp
(Part of the President's Disaster Management
    Egov Initiative)
(800) 451-2647
Web site: http://disasterhelp.gov/portal/jhtml/index.jhtml

Federal Emergency Management Agency (FEMA)
500 C Street SW
Washington, DC 20472
(800) 480-2520
Web site: http://www.fema.gov

Multidisciplinary Center for Earthquake Engineering
    Research (MCEER)
Red Jacket Quadrangle
Buffalo, NY 14261
(716) 645-3391
Web site: http://mceer.buffalo.edu

National Weather Service (NWS)
1325 East West Highway
Silver Spring, MD 20910
(301) 713-0224
Web site: http://www.nws.noaa.gov

U.S. Geological Survey (USGS)
National Center
12201 Sunrise Valley Drive
Reston, VA 20192
(888) ASK-USGS (275-8747)
Web site: http://www.usgs.gov

Web Sites

Due to the changing nature of Internet links, the Rosen
Publishing Group, Inc., has developed an online list of
Web sites related to the subject of this book. This site is
updated regularly. Please use this link to access the list:

http://www.rosenlinks.com/lep/eart

For Further Reading

Ball, Jackie, et al. *Earthquakes* (Our Planet Earth).
    Milwaukee, WI: Gareth Stevens Publishing, 2004.
Colson, Mary. *Shaky Ground: Earthquakes* (Turbulent
    Planet). Chicago, IL: Raintree, 2004.
Mehta-Jones, Shilpa. *Earthquake Alert!* (Disaster Alert!).
    New York, NY: Crabtree Publishing Company, 2004.
Moores, Eldridge M, ed. *Volcanoes and Earthquakes*
    (Discoveries). New York, NY: Barnes and Noble Books, 2003.
Morris, Neil. *Earthquakes* (The Wonders of Our World).
    New York, NY: Crabtree Publishing Company, 1998.
Murray, Peter. *Earthquakes* (Forces of Nature). Chanhassen,
    MN: The Child's World, Inc., 1999.
Nicholson, Cynthia Pratt. *Earthquakes.* Tonawanda, NY: Kids
    Can Press, 2002.
Richards, Julie. *Quivering Quakes* (Natural Disasters).
    Broomall, PA: Chelsea House Publishers, 2001.
Spigarelli, Jack A. *Crisis Preparedness Handbook: A Complete
    Guide to Home Storage and Physical Survival.* Alpine, UT:
    Cross-Current Publishing, 2002.
Sutherland, Lin. *Earthquakes and Volcanoes* (Reader's
    Digest Pathfinders). Pleasantville, NY: Reader's Digest
    Children's Publishing, Inc., 2000.
Trueit, Trudi Strain. *Earthquakes* (Watts Library). New York,
    NY: Franklin Watts, 2003.

Van Rose, Susanna. *Volcanoes and Earthquakes* (Eyewitness). New York, NY: Dorling Kindersley, 2004.

"Your Evacuation Plan." American Red Cross. Retrieved August 15, 2005 (http://www.redcross.org/services/ disaster/0,1082,0_6_,00.html).

Bibliography

Brown, Ian. "All Shook Up." *Saturday Night*, April 1994, p. 32.

Buis, Alan, et al. "NASA Details Earthquake Effects on the Earth." NASA Jet Propulsion Laboratory, January 10, 2005. Retrieved June 12, 2005 (http://www.jpl.nasa.gov/news/news.cfm?release=2005-009).

Federal Emergency Management Agency. "What You Might Feel in a Disaster." FEMA for Kids. Retrieved June 12, 2005 (http://www.fema.gov/kids/feel.htm).

Grace, Catherine O'Neill. *The Forces of Nature: The Awesome Power of Volcanoes, Earthquakes, and Tornadoes.* Washington, DC: National Geographic, 2004.

Lassieur, Allison. *Earthquakes.* San Diego, CA: Lucent Books, 2002.

National Earthquake Hazards Reduction Program. Retrieved June 12, 2005 (http://www.training.fema.gov/emiweb/EarthQuake/index.htm).

NOAA. "NOAA Reacts Quickly to Indonesian Tsunami." Retrieved June 12, 2005 (http://www.noaanews.noaa.gov/stories2004/s2357.htm).

Rao, Paula, and Dr. Lucy Jones. "Earthquake ABC," 1994. Retrieved June 12, 2005 (http://pasadena.wr.usgs.gov/ABC).

Trueit, Trudi Strain. *Earthquakes.* New York, NY: Franklin Watts, 2003.

U.S. Geological Survey. "Cool Earthquake Facts." Retrieved February 25, 2005 (http://earthquake.usgs.gov/4kids/facts.html).

Wikipedia. "2004 Indian Ocean Earthquake." Retrieved June 12, 2005 (http://en.wikipedia.org/wiki/2004_Indian_Ocean_earthquake).

Yeats, Robert R. *Living with Earthquakes in California: A Survivor's Guide.* Corvallis, OR: Oregon State University Press, 2001.

Index

About the Authors

Suzanne J. Murdico was a writer and researcher who wrote more than twenty books for children and teens. She was born and raised in Levittown, Pennsylvania, and became interested in the history of natural disasters after she and her husband, Vinnie, moved to Wesley Chapel, Florida, and experienced their first hurricanes there. Ms. Murdico worked for the publishing industry for more than twenty years, including in the development of textbooks, teachers' materials, and ancillaries for elementary through the college level.

Greg Roza has an MA in English. He is a writer and an editor who works a for a publisher of educational texts for children. Mr. Roza's interest in researching natural disasters and emergency preparedness stems from his childhood growing up in western New York, where he and his family experienced yearly blizzards that often brought their community to a standstill for days on end.

Photo Credits

Cover, p. 1 © Roger Ressmeyer/Corbis; pp. 5, 12, 14, 19, 21, 22, 30, 37, 38, 40, 46, 49, 51 © AP/ Wide World Photos; p. 10 courtesy of the United States Geological Survey, Earthquake Hazards Program; p. 13 courtesy of the United States Geological Survey; p. 27 courtesy of the Washington State Department of Health; p. 35 courtesy of Federal Emergency Management Agency: National Earthquakes Hazard Reduction Program; p. 43, 50, 52 courtesy of FEMA.

Designer: Tahara Anderson; Editor: Kathy Kuhtz Campbell